MR
TOPSY-TURVY

by Roger Hargreaves

WORLD INTERNATIONAL
MANCHESTER

Mr Topsy Turvy was a funny sort of a fellow.

Everything about him was either upside down, or inside out, or back to front — topsy turvy in fact.

It was all very extraordinary!

To give you some idea of how topsy turvy Mr Topsy Turvy was, you ought to see his house.

The front door is upside down to start with.

And the curtains hang upside down at the windows.

And just look at that chimney pot!

All very extraordinary!

Inside is the same.

Just look at the clock standing on Mr Topsy Turvy's mantlepiece.

Isn't that the topsiest turviest clock you've ever seen?

And just look at the way Mr Topsy Turvy reads a book.

Not only does he read it upside down, but he starts to read it at the back page!

And just look where Mr Topsy Turvy puts the stamp when he sends a letter to somebody.

Have you ever seen anything like it?

Mr Smith
High Street
The Town

Now, this story is all about the time Mr Topsy Turvy came to the town where you and I live.

Nobody is quite sure how Mr Topsy Turvy got there, or where he came from, but he did arrive, because somebody saw him getting off the train.

The trouble was, he did it in a topsy turvy way, and got out the wrong side and fell on to the railway line.

Which really isn't all that surprising, is it?

When he'd picked himself up and managed to find his way out of the station, Mr Topsy Turvy went to a hotel to find a room to spend the night.

The hotel manager tried not to smile when he saw Mr Topsy Turvy walk into his hotel carrying his suitcase upside down and with his topsy turvy hat on his head.

"Good afternoon, sir," he said. "Can I help you?"

Now, something you didn't know about Mr Topsy Turvy is the way he speaks.

You see, he sometimes gets things the wrong way round.

"Afternoon good," said Mr Topsy Turvy to the hotel manager. "I'd room a like!"

The manager scratch his head. "You mean you'd like a room?" he asked.

"Please yes," replied Mr Topsy Turvy.

Eventually the hotel manager managed to work out what Mr Topsy Turvy was talking about, and he was taken up in the lift to a bedroom.

Then Mr Topsy Turvy unpacked his suitcase, put on his pyjamas, and went to bed.

He was rather tired after travelling from wherever he'd come from.

The following day Mr Topsy Turvy went round the town.

But what a fuss his going round the town caused.

He took a taxi from the hotel, but so confused the taxi driver trying to tell him where he wanted to go, the poor man drove straight into a traffic light.

"Oh dear," said Mr Topsy Turvy. "I am sorry very!"

Then he went into a big department store in the middle of the town.

He walked up to one of the counters.

"I'd like a sock of pairs," he said to the lady behind the counter.

"You mean a pair of socks," she smiled, and showed him a pair of bright red socks.

Mr Tospy Turvy put them on his hands!

Then he tried to leave, but being Mr Topsy Turvy he tried to walk down the up escalator, and all the people who were going up the up escalator all fell over themselves.

It was a terrible topsy turvy jumble!

That day Mr Topsy Turvy did all sorts of topsy turvy things.

He walked backwards across a street crossing, and caused an enormous traffic jam.

He went to a library and put all the books upside down on the shelves, and made everybody extremely cross.

Then he went to an art gallery and insisted on hanging all the pictures upside down so that he could look at them properly.

And then, after Mr Topsy Turvy had been in the town for just one day, he disappeared.

Nobody knew how he went, or where he went, but he certainly went because he wasn't there any more.

The whole town breathed a sigh of relief.

But . . .

What the town discovered, even though Mr Topsy Turvy had left, was that everything was still topsy turvy.

"Read all it about," shouted the newspaper sellers, instead of shouting, "Read all about it".

"News is the here," said the television newsreader, instead of saying, "Here is the news".

"Morning good," people started saying to each other when they met, and "Do do you how?" instead of, "How do you do?".

Everybody was talking topsy turvy!

Can you think of something to say that's topsy turvy?

Go on, try!